UNEXPECTED

by
Prince E. Mayes-Sullivan

Love Unexpected
by Prince E. Mayes-Sullivan

Edited by: Rhyan Neco

ISBN: Print: 978-0-9975833-1-1
             Ebook: 978-0-9975833-1-1

Printed and Published in the United States of America

First Printing 2018

Table of Contents

Love Unexpected

INTRODUCTION:
Love in the Beginning

They lay together in the heat of the moment, tensions high, bodies sweating, hearts pounding. It was the beginning of a mystifying night. Scared yet excited, passionate yet strong, love in the beginning can never be wrong. In a room just big enough for two, they started to connect in a way that felt inhuman. As they began on an unknown path they'd never before seen, it became clear they were no longer in control. The fight to gain back that control slowly died and the tears in their eyes became proof of inseparable love. Suddenly, His hands began to slide around her neck. While still making love, he beat her head in, again, and again, until... blood crawled like snakes slithering down the wall and onto the bed.

She was quick to get undressed. She was overcome as her soul mate entered her. Screams of love were released. Just when she thought it was over, another thrust was given. As her brain entered a tizzy, she couldn't help but think, 'Damn, she's good!' She surrendered to the love her passionate partner delivered. If only she'd known it would be for the last time.

He started slow, his purpose was to please. His partner moaned as he pleasured him in a way no one else could. The repeated motion made them both hot. Wanting the same outcome, they worked together to feel, build a climax, simply make love. But, a problem occurred—a problem they couldn't see or feel. Pleasure slowly turned to pain. The two stopped as they felt the presence of someone lurking. He was yanked from the car. They both screamed in panic. And one suddenly started gasping for air. Then it was over . . . dead!

PART ONE

Chapter One: The First Audition

Audition ~

AUDITION TODAY AT 4 PM!

Nick read the notice and knew he had to go. Nick was a six-foot-four, muscular male, with a complexion that reminded you of a fresh-baked apple pie crust, light but not too dark, the kind your grandmother use to bake. It was just right! Nick, a minor league baseball player who'd jumped into the acting scene, was excited about the audition.

He hopped out of his Suburban truck, rubbed his hands together, then wiped them on his pants. Nervous sweat. He immediately ran towards the door to the building when he realized it was already 3:55 PM. He was in such a hurry, he forgot to lock his doors. Nick realized the auditions weren't in a city like Buckhead so he ran back and hit his alarm on the keyring. A single honk from his horn sounded, signifying the doors were locked. He walked toward the door again, hitting his alarm two more times just to be sure.

Nick entered the building and stopped at the front desk to sign in. He was greeted by an older woman wearing glasses that rested on the tip of her nose. He noticed her wig was tilted to the side, and just as he was going to say something to her about it, she greeted him. "Sign in, young man, and go have a seat inside the room to your left."

Nick stood there for a second to see if she would react to his gorgeous appearance.

She looked up at him again and asked, "Do you have a question?"

"Oh, uh, No, ma'am", he responded. You said inside the room to the left?" "What? I didn't speak loud enough for you the first time?"

He stopped rubbing his hands together and walked into the almost-empty audition space. The room was old, hot, and muggy. The only people left were unemployed, struggling actors. As he looked for a place to sit, he eyed a caramel-skinned, brown-eyed girl. Not knowing anything about her, or if he had a chance, he sat next to her and attempted to make conversation.

"Auditions remind me of the first day of baseball tryouts," Nick said nervously, rubbing his hands together as his palms began to sweat once again.

"It's simple." she replied nonchalantly, looking at her sides.

"How so?" asked Nick.

"Well, you just have to be yourself. That's what they're looking for," She looked up from her sides to notice his nervous, yet extremely sexy demeanor.

"By the way, I'm Nikole." She quickly introduced herself.

"Excuse me, I'm Nick. I just moved here from Cincinnati, Ohio."

Nikole took a moment to study him. "You look more like a New Yorker."

Nick laughed a bit. "I wish," he said, smiling at the idea. "So, you go to a lot of these?"

"Yeah, I have to. This is my only job besides modeling. A girl's gotta eat." She laughed a little, showing her breathtaking smile.

Nick chuckled. "A model? That's wassup! I grew up doing photography when I wasn't on a baseball field."

"That explains the muscles. I'm always looking for photographers. Have you connected with any studios?"

"Only my studio apartment," Nick replied sarcastically but very serious. "But if I can help you, I'd be more than willing."

"Name your price."

"Connections."

"And?"

"That's it."

"There has to be more," Nikole said, still suspect. "A date?" "NIKOLE BATES!" the audition assistant called.

Nikole tore off a piece of paper, wrote her number on it, and handed it to Nick without saying a word. After gathering her belongings, she proceeded to the audition room. Nick saved her number in his phone.

Later that night Nick opened the car door for Nikole. The two entered the Apache Atlanta Night Club. They surrounded themselves in the free-spirited atmosphere. Nikole was fully immersed in the old, familiar place, while Nick was a bit uneasy and on edge.

"This is where everyone gets together," Nikole said. "Actors, singers, directors, drag queens . . ."

"Seems interesting," Nick stated sincerely.

The two found their way to a round booth for a more intimate setting. Nikole saw Nick put both hands in his pockets.

"Nervous?"

"Sorta."

"Don't be. It's a very laid-back, yet busy city." Pointing out two drag queens, Nikole reiterated her point. "A place where anything goes . . . lovely."

"Don't see a whole lot of that in Cincinnati."

"No gay friends?"

"Not really. Just a gay sister and brother. In a way, I was the odd child. The only thing my siblings and I have in common is our love for performing."

"Nothing wrong with that. In this town, different is the norm."

"You from here?"

Nikole's expression deflated. "I'm from California."

"And you moved here to start a career in entertainment?"

"I know it sounds insane, but for a young black actress and model, Atlanta is where it's at." Her mood lightened up a bit.

"I'm here because I can't afford to stay in New York or California." Nick laughed. "But, like you said, this seems like the hot spot for Black Hollywood."

The two ordered drinks and continued talking, so much so they were two of the very few left in the almost deserted club.

"That's a wrap tonight, y'all," the host announced on the mic. "Come back and jam with us tomorrow night."

"That's our cue, I guess," Nick said, finishing up his final drink for the evening.

"I don't know why, but I feel this strong connection to you," Nikole said, sipping what was left of her drink. "I usually don't do this, but can I come to your apartment?"

"I haven't really had a chance to fix it up," Nick said hesitantly. He sensed something that was familiar to him. When he was younger, his post adolescence made him a sex symbol during high school. He knew at that point she wanted him. Without overthinking it, he replied, "You know what? Sure!"

The newly-formed couple headed to Nikole's car. She threw the keys to him.

"Let's see what ya got, Nick. You know your way home, sir?" Nikole asked when they got in the car.

"It's straight down 285."

Chapter Two: Strange Love

On the outskirts of L.A., a young, eager couple unpacked their belongings. They lived in a rough neighborhood. The two had just rented a very modest two-bedroom, one-bathroom apartment. Though the couple didn't have much, they had hope—even if half the world and one of their parents found it to be an abomination before God. Marquis was a sexy, light-skinned sensitive guy, a Cancer. While he unpacked, he spent some time on the phone with his godmother Deborah, who he considered to be his mother. Although he found her annoying at times, he let her offer her sometimes smothering, yet useful advice. All in all, he was a mama's boy. As for his father......well, it was complicated.

"It's my mother," he said, holding the phone up. "She acts like we've never moved before." He put the phone back to his mouth. "We have it under control, Ma."

"Tell Ma I said hi," Mario chimed in.

Mario was five-eight with chocolate skin pretty enough to want to eat. He saw the good in all situations, and he knew how to calm his partner down—not only sexually, but physically and mentally....

"Mario says hi . . . She sends her love," Marquis said, annoyed that he was unpacking and on the phone at the same time. "Mom, I have to go. Love you too, bye." Marquis let out a sigh of relief.

"Someone seems relieved," Mario said, seeing Marquis was getting quite flustered. "Honey, it's okay. We made it. We have our own place."

"I know, but we still have so much to do. All we have is a couch and—"

"Baby, we're going to be okay, just take it one day at a time" Mario cut Marquis off. "Things will fall into place, Marqi," Mario reassured.

"I know. I-I just want the best for us."

Mario and Marquis had been together for over three years. Both wanting nothing more than acceptance in the world, they clung to each other like two magnets. Marquis was a starving actor and model, looking for his big break in Hollywood. He worked part-time as a tour guide at Universal Studios, mainly to stay connected in the entertainment business and to meet people who could help make him millions. While Mario was in school for psychology, he often took modeling jobs with Marquis to help with the living expenses.

Both of their families lived in different states. Not having much money, they picked one holiday every year to visit family, alternating families each year. Mario often tried not to go to his family's house because of the strained relationship with his father. Mario Senior had a difficult time accepting his son's homosexuality because of his so-ocalled alignment with nature. He believed that since two men cannot procreate, homosexuality was unnatural and therefore blasphemous. Because Mario's father had been such an outlier to his life, he often encouraged Marquis to talk to his father Tyrone. It's often easier to fix someone else's problem than to fix your own, as was the case here.

కు ♦ స

A few days had passed and Marquis was in the kitchen cooking breakfast while Mario prepared for his morning classes. Mario came into the kitchen.

"Hey, sexy," Marquis said in a very deep tone of voice, "I cooked your favorite." Marquis held a plate of scrambled eggs with cheese, sausage links, buttered wheat toast, and a glass of OJ.

"Thanks, Marqi," Mario said, attempting to hold him, "but I want something else."

Mario started to kiss his neck. Marquis giggled as he sat the plate of food down. Mario pulled down his partner's pants and received a different type of food. The two stumbled to the living room, pulling each other's clothes off. It was time for Marquis to enjoy his 'chocolate bar'. Mario moaned with pleasure, causing Marquis to moan louder. Suddenly a phone alarm sounded.

"Time for class."

"But I want some ass!" Marquis pouted.

"Later," Mario rubbed Marqi's hard-on, "I'll give you that and so much more." He picked up his school bag, walked out the door, and got into his Uber.

Marquis sat all alone and lonely. He pulled out his phone and scrolled through the apps. He stumbled upon an app he thought he'd deleted—a gay dating site, or in his mind, the 'forbidden'. But lonely and somewhat aroused, he started to scroll through hundreds of sexy men, until someone from the app messaged him. Marquis didn't see the harm in a little chatting. Oh, but he was so wrong!

Chapter Three: Big City/Little Money

New York, the Big Apple—a place where dreams come true. Or, a place where actors work three jobs, a murky figure robs you in the heart of Times Square, and a common place to get mugged is on the ride home in a subway train. But to newlyweds Kortney and Koko, it was home. Kortney and Kaira 'Koko' Evans had just rented a cozy place in the Bronx in a mediocre neighborhood— in other words, a rat infested, ghetto neighbor, and somewhat violent apartment building—with two tiny bedrooms and a bathroom smaller than most closets. But Kortney's lifelong dream of being a Broadway star kept her wanting to live in New York. Kortney, coming home from an audition for a new Broadway show, caught the subway then had a twenty-minute walk home. With Kortney not having the best self-esteem, she entered the small apartment with her head hung low. Koko, a heavy-set girl with a faded bob sporting purple-and-orange highlights and tattoos everywhere, was sitting in her tiny table top studio. All of the equipment Koko used had been stolen. She had just finished recording a few bars of a rap she had written.

"How'd the audition go?" Koko asked, already knowing the answer.

"It went." Kortney plopped down on the couch. "I'm not what they're looking for. I never am."

"No, they don't know what they're lookin' for." Koko went to hold her.

"The casting director asked for a blow job!"

"What did you say to him?" Koko slowly asked angrily.

"I don't need this gig!" She glanced at the pile of bills stacked on their small coffee table.

"Don't worry babe, my career's 'bout to blow up." Koko considered herself one of the greatest rappers of all time no one had heard of—yet.

Kortney just shook her head, wanting to believe in Koko's career, but it just wasn't looking good. "Babe, trust me . . . we gon be good," Koko reassured her.

Coming to NYC, the couple hadn't realized how tough it would be living in one of the most expensive cities in America. With Kortney not having a family that was well off, there was no one to borrow from. And with Koko not having a stable family during her childhood, being tossed around from foster home to foster home, she was even less well off than Kortney. As a child, Koko had trouble keeping to herself and got punished for doing "strange" things to other foster kids in the different homes she lived in. Not knowing where she came from made Koko a bitter woman. However, like everyone else, love kept Koko happy.

It was 3 AM and Koko had just left Club Groove on 125 MacDougal Street in Manhattan. She would often go to open-mic night to get feedback on her lyrics and flow. With Groove being so small, and everyone knowing each other on the music scene, Koko was confident that no one would think of biting her rhymes. She felt at home, she felt free to create, and with Kortney not being able to go with her, she felt free to mingle. Girls threw themselves at

Koko on this particular night, left and right. It was Koko's night. When it was all over however, Koko was going home to Kortney. Once outside of the venue, anyone could see that it was not in an area safe enough for someone to walk home alone, especially a female. But Koko always kept her head on a swivel. When she thought the coast was clear, she started to walk toward the subway. What she didn't know was someone had followed her—someone she never needed to cross paths with.

Chapter Four: When Fools Fall in Love

Nick and Nikole had been living together in Nick's apartment for four months now. The once-empty studio was now filled with tons of stuff. The apartment was now like a maze, the walls consisting of all of Nikole's belongings. She could feel the potential Nick had as a partner, and wanted very badly for them to be together, no matter the cost. Nick didn't seem to care about the untidiness. He'd been able to network with powerful people in Atlanta and had great sex with Nikole. He gave her shelter, and she gave him connections and good head, so why would Nick complain? The two were in bed, just finishing a lust-filled session.

"Damn, yo you put that work in!" Nick stretched and headed to the bathroom.

Nikole sat up straight on the twin-size mattress, neon green lace bra still on. Something heavy had been on her mind. Nick had yet to clarify whether the two of them were an official couple. Nikole quietly, and desperately craved that clarity and went about getting it the only way she knew how.

"You know I've been thinking?" With hesitation, she continued. "You never talk about your family.

Why not?"

"It isn't important," he answered in a nonchalant way. "They're complicated personalities. We're very competitive of each other!" he said, with a sense of finality as he came from the bathroom.

With the Thanksgiving holiday a few weeks away, Nikole had a surprise for Nick. "Don't get mad but—" She threw him the phone which had two airline confirmations on the screen. Every ounce of energy drained from his soul. His hands were now soaked in sweat. "Isn't that exciting?" Nikole asked.

Nick slowly and calmly approached Nikole, then suddenly slapped-the-shit out of her and choked her up against the wall. Nick relived his childhood in those few moments— he relived watching his father abuse women. So much overwhelmed him at that moment that he blacked out.

When Nick was eleven years old, he'd come home from baseball practice early one day and spotted his father in the garage with another woman. Nick, at that age, knew it wasn't right. Trying not to make his presence known, he peeked through a hole in the garage door. Fully engaged in the sexual encounter, his father was oblivious to the fact someone could see him, but the woman felt Nick's presence.

"TYRONE, STOP!" she screamed and pointed at the hole.

"Bitch!" Mad his enjoyment had come to a halt, Tyrone slapped-the-shit out of her.

For the first time, Nick's palms began to sweat. That moment traumatized Nick for life, causing him to have anger and betrayal issues as a growing adolescent.

After a few moments had passed, Nick was back in his reality. He could feel the hurt and see the pain on Nikole's face he'd put there. Nikole, on the verge of tears, consoled herself internally, scared that any emotion would set off his anger again. It wasn't the first time he'd abused her. Nick felt he really needed to keep her, therefore, he scared her into staying. The fear Nick instilled within Nikole prompted her to pay the bills, and ultimately, take care of him and his needs. At this point, she was scared to leave. Not being able to deal with the aftermath, Nick went for a walk. As soon as he left, Nikole let her pain out and wept until she fell asleep.

Nick came back from his walk almost five hours later. He had a way of getting out of things. Most of the time, he pretended like it had never happened. But after this particular event, he wasn't sure if he could redeem himself. Nikole was shaken by Nick's appearance when he walked in. He held food in his hands.

"You straight?" he asked with his head hung low. "I brought food from our favorite spot." Nikole, at that moment, realized her critical mistake. She had never learned who Nick really was. From the outside, he was talented, smart, and fine. But what about his family, past relationships, and more importantly, his mental status?

Again, she decided to move past the abusive act. They sat down on the couch and started eating the food Nick had brought. After twenty minutes, the silence was broken.

"I thought about it, and you're right, it's time." Nikole was puzzled by Nick's statement.

"Time for what?" she asked.

"For you to meet my family." He smiled. "Dad will like you . . . if he is in a good mood."

Nikole got the hint that they weren't going to talk about the previous events. She was scared as fuck!

Chapter Five: My Wants, Desires, and Needs

For the past few months, Mario had been consumed with school. So much so, that he hadn't even realized Marquis had bought little things to make the apartment feel more like their home. Marquis was happy his man was doing so well in school, but at the same time, he felt neglected. He had begun to talk to different guys on a dating app just for socialization. Marquis felt bad at first, but he needed the attention.

"Hey, I have a study group tonight. I'll be late, Marqi," Mario said, heading out the door. Marquis' phone vibrated. It was an app notification.

Terrell9587 sent you a message, his phone read.

Hesitant, he opened the app and started a conversation. They both revealed very personal things about themselves— not so much sexual, but their wants, desires, and needs. Marquis was now getting the attention he wanted, but it would come at a price.

Because of his new friend Terrell, Marquis was late for his audition. When he entered the lavish L.A. casting room, he could feel the heat of frustration from the casting directors.

"I apologize for being late." Marquis scrambled to get the words out. "L.A. traffic, gotta love it," he said jokingly.

An assistant handed him the side of a script.

"Read the part of Terrell," one casting director said.

Marquis was shocked by the name and just stood there for a few moments.

"I SAID, GO AHEAD!" the director yelled.

Marquis read the side and finished the audition. With a couple of hours to spare before his next audition, he thought about Mario, wishing he wasn't so busy. With no family in town, he turned to his new friend Terrell, who was more than happy to meet in person.

Terrell and Marquis met at the Tuesday Night Café, a nice, small place to hear great live entertainment. Mixed with a variety of people, Marquis wasn't as apprehensive as he had been at first. Terrell was tall and masculine with dreads, his skin cocoa brown, with black-and-red gauges in his ears. The two talked about everything—their families, partners, and careers.

Terrell was in his second year of law school, with an interest in entertainment law. With Marquis trying to get in the entertainment industry, he took ear to who and what Terrell knew. Within thirty minutes, they had talked about the industry, living in L.A., and Marquis had even told Terrell he hadn't had sex in two months. Needless to say, Terrell felt sorry for him. "Does he really love you?" Terrell asked.

"Yes, it's just school." Marquis sighed. "It takes so much out of him, but he's doing so well."

"Yeah, but two months?" Terrell shook his head. "That's a long time!"

"Thank God for porn," Marquis said jokingly.

"You know they say porn can lower your sex drive".

"You sound like a psychologist; my boyfriend is in school for psychology."

"Oh yeah, I love getting in people's heads too!"

More time passed as the two continued to chat about life. Eventually, Marquis had to leave for his gig. Terrell paid the bill and slipped Marquis his number before he left.

Headed to his modeling gig, Marquis couldn't believe how ironic his day had been. He felt bad he'd enjoyed himself so much. He entered Terrell's number in his phone as L.A. Cast 9587. The next moment he received a phone call. His phone read, "My Bae". It was Mario.

"Hey, Marqi, I was just checkin' on you. I'll be home early tonight, don't cook."

"Why not?"

"I'm taking you out."

"Where?"

"It's a surprise, Marqi!"

"Okay. I'm headed to a shoot. I should be done around eight."

"Great! Be ready. Love you, bye."

"Love you too," Marquis said, walking into his photo shoot.

Later that night, Marquis and Mario got into the car. Mario still wouldn't give the secret location away, but as Marquis looked at his surroundings, he started to worry. They pulled up to . . . the Tuesday Night Café.

"Surprise! You've been saying how you wanted to come here for the longest!"

Marquis' face dropped. Putting it off as surprise, he discreetly put a cap over his head so the employees wouldn't see the repeat customer. Mario was oblivious to Marquis's murmuring prayers asking God to make sure no one remembered him from his lunchtime rendezvous. As Marquis' nerves settled down when no one let out his secret, dinner was delicious! The two made it a point not to talk about work or school—only their relationship. Marquis made it a point to put his phone on Do Not Disturb.

"I have a surprise," Mario said excitedly. "I thought about it and maybe . . . it's time to visit Cincinnati."

He reached for his bag and pulled out two plane tickets. "We're going to visit Tyrone for the holiday."

The blood flushed from Marquis' face.

Chapter Six: Pray the Predator Away

The night Koko left Club Groove, she met the woman who would become her escape, but also her biggest regret. Twenty-three-year-old Tanya had the body of an angel—tall, light skinned, with red Remy weave flowing down to her lower back. She was an up and coming singer, trying to make some strides in the industry. Koko always boasted about different connections while she was out, and this one was going to put her to the test. Tanya sat next to Koko on the train that night and sparked a never-ending conversation.

"Hi. I don't mean to bother you, but your lyrics are amazing," Tanya complimented Koko.

"You're pretty dope yourself. What's your name?" Koko asked.

"Tanya, but I go by Tangya."

"Different. I like different."

"I like different too. I just moved here from Jamaica Queens about two months ago," Tanya said.

"I was told that Groove was the place for artists," she continued.

"Yeah. It's a great spot. You never know who'll be there."

"You go every week?"

"I try to. My wife and I live in the Bronx, but that doesn't bother me."

Tanya seemed surprised. "You're taken. What a shame."

"Her name is Kortney. She's an actress."

"Broadway?"

"Right now, off-Broadway, but Broadway is the main goal."

"Oh, okay," Tanya said, not really interested in Kortney. "How about you?"

"I book gigs here and there. Lookin' for something more steady."

"Looks should be your last problem," Tanya said coming on to Koko. "This is me."

When the train stopped, Tanya slipped Koko her number and walked out into the empty New York subway station.

When Koko finally made it home, it was almost 4AM. Koko walked into the apartment as

Kortney was studying a script. She knew there was a problem with her getting home so late and not calling.

"You're home!" Kortney said sarcastically.

"I know it's late, bae, but you know how we get down."

"I do. That's why you need to check in." Kortney stared deeply into Koko's soul with piercing eyes.

"I'M sorry, bae." She sat down next to her. "I'll make it up."

"See, that's your problem," Kortney said, starting to get frustrated. "You think you can fix everything with the flick of your tongue!"

"I mean," Koko said, feeling the sarcastic comment.

"You aren't helping your case!" Kortney sat up on the couch. "I hope you had fun, because you aren't getting anything tonight. Plus, we have to start saving up for Ohio."

"We're really going to Tyrone's for Thanksgiving?"

"Yes indeed we are."

"Great! Just fucking great!!" Koko plopped down on the couch.

For Koko, revisiting Ohio was like being put back into a pit of fire. As a young girl, Koko's foster parents showed the opposite of compassion. Koko's foster father showed his love by being a very strict and physical disciplinarian. This caused Koko to feel like no one in the world cared about her for a very long time. Koko knew she'd have to suck it up and go home, but there was no way she was going to visit her last toxic foster family who beat her. She wasn't about to be around people who didn't give a shit about her. Not even for a second.

When Kortney first met Koko, they were neighbors. Koko hadn't thought about being with girls—at least that's the story she stuck to—but when she met Kortney, her inner self was free. For the first time, she felt comfortable in her skin. Now this time, it was Kortney who was in for an unexpected surprise.

PART TWO

Chapter Seven: The Family Meets Up

Now all in baggage claim, the three siblings spotted each other. Eager to see how everyone was doing, they ran in tandem to embrace their family. They were happy to see each other, yet a little envious of each other as well. Nick was in the Hotlanta scene, Marquis in the entertainment capital, and Kortney lived just miles from the Great White Way. In some way, everyone would be more than willing to swap lives for a day.

"So, what have my little sis and bro-bro been up to?" Nick, the oldest sibling, asked.

"The question is: What have you been up to?" Kortney and Marquis asked in unison, wondering who the woman was who accompanied him.

"My bad, this is my friend Nikole," Nick said, introducing her to the family. Nikole gave a faint "Hello," while the sting of the title 'friend' rattled in her brain.

Everyone introduced themselves, but Kortney caught something interesting about Nikole, a secret of some sort, and with that, questions started to flow. She was trying to figure out why Nikole had on sunglasses on this late November evening.

"So, Nikole, what do you do?" Kortney asked with digging curiosity.

"Well, I'm an actress and a model," she responded, with a hint of sadness and fear.

"How about we head to Tyrone's place?" Mario said, sensing Nikole's apprehension.

The six hopped on a bus to take them to the place where Nick, Kortney, and Marquis grew up. Growing up had been rough on the three. Their parents divorced when they were young. Cecily, their mother, had been in and out of her children's lives. She'd had enough of their father's cheating, and ended up running off with someone close to the family. Nick, Marquis, and Kortney often wondered why their mother left them behind.

When they arrived at their childhood home, all three siblings had different feelings that began to surface—confusion, animosity, and hope—all caused by their parents. Now their partners were going to see firsthand, the backstory to their lovers' lives. This was especially big for Nikole, being the new girl. How would Tyrone receive her, and why did Nick's mom leave? But Nikole wasn't the only one in for a surprise. Tyrone was an interesting man. He wasn't big on being flashy. His only vice was 'loving' women a little too much. Other than that, he was cool— except when he was angry. One thing you didn't want to do, was upset Tyrone.

He had kept a vital secret from his children about this particular holiday visit, a secret that was going to change everyone.

Chapter Eight: Where the Drama Began

December 2, 1999—the day Cecily left. She'd had enough of Tyrone's conspicuous attraction to other women, and Cecily was a woman of revenge. While Nick and Marquis were away at school and Kortney was at her Godmother Deborah's daycare, Cecily decided to invite Tyrone's brother Richard over just before Tyrone was expected back. When Richard walked in, she called him to the bedroom, greeting him in her lace panties and heels. Richard earned his money as a stockbroker. He always had nice clothes, but he had never been a ladies' man. You could say he envied Tyrone's luck with the ladies, so he was more than willing to get a piece of his brother's wife.

Richard entered the bedroom and stared at his sexy sister-in-law in her naked, laced glory as the Isley Brothers "In Between the Sheets" played. They both knew it was about to go down! "Come here, daddy," Cecily said as she kicked her heels off and slowly pulled the lace panties down. "It's time to shine!" "YES, IT IS!" Richard shouted.

They entered a sexual twilight zone. Moaning, groping, and cursing were just some of the activities that transpired. Cecily was so good, Richard forgot his brother was on the way home. The two weren't worried about it, but they should have been.

Tyrone pulled up a couple of minutes into their love session. But not alone. Tyrone had a 'regular' with him. As he walked in, he and his girl heard the sounds of love being made. With Tyrone being a man of his caliber, he carried a gun with him at all times. He immediately ran upstairs with his 'Magnum' cap pistol and entered the room. Full rage took over as he watched his brother make love to his woman. He fired a shot.

"What-the-fuck is going on in my house?" Tyrone raged. "Revenge!" Cecily said, riding Richard. Tyrone fired a shot at Richard. The bullet grazed the side of his chest. Tyrone's friend entered the room.

"Who-the-hell is she?!" Cecily asked, outraged.

They both knew they were in the wrong. How would their children take it at such a young age? Cecily eventually decided it was best to move in with Richard and gave Tyrone full custody of the kids. Neither Tyrone nor Cecily ever explained what happened to their children, but now with them being adults, Tyrone decided the truth should finally come out.

Chapter Nine: The Truth Shall Set Us Free

The six of them walked into Tyrone's home. His place was a mood, a full out 1980's groove. The 'mood' brought up memories of the mid-nineties. They could recall the joy of opening gifts on the old couch protected in plastic, they remembered the crazy lamp with five lights that hung in the corner, and even felt the sadness caused by their mother's abandonment. Their lovers had different feelings. For them, they could now imagine the stories their partners had told so frequently. Nikole had a lot of questions but was afraid to ask. The floor creaked as 48-year-old Tyrone strolled down the old carpeted steps.

"Dad!" Kortney said excitedly as she ran to hug him. "I've missed you!"

"I've missed you too, princess." He looked at his boys. "You two haven't changed. Nick, who's the young lady?"

"This is Nikole, Dad," Nick introduced his 'friend'. "We've been together a few months." "Nice to meet you—"

"Call me Tyrone." He said, cutting Nikole off as he hugged her. "Mario, Kaira, how've you two been?"

"Things are going well, sir," Mario replied, answering his question. "Good to get a way for a bit."

"How about you, Kaira?"

"I'm out here grindin' like everyone else," Koko said with a laugh.

That left Marquis. Marquis and Tyrone's relationship had been strained, to say the least. Not because of Marquis's sexuality, but because of the role his father had played in his mother's disappearance. In Marquis's mind, if it hadn't been for Tyrone's notorious cases of infidelity, his mom may have stayed with him.

"Son?" Tyrone looked at Marquis. "It's good to see you." "You too," Marquis replied, slightly annoyed.

Mario sensed something was up with Marquis. To avoid the problem at hand, he distracted the others from the father-son drama that was playing out.

"I smell your famous chili and corn muffins," Mario said, pointing out the smell of red and black beans, and a variety of spices and seasonings.

The dysfunctional family entered the dining room. When Tyrone went towards the kitchen, he was stopped by Kortney.

"I'll get it, Dad." She smiled at Nikole, "Wanna help me?"

A little puzzled, Nikole replied, "Sure."

The two left the men and Koko to talk about a multitude of current events. As the two entered the kitchen, Nikole's nerves shot up—so much that Kortney felt it.

"What has my brother been doing to you?"

"What makes you say something like that?" Nikole asked, trying to hide the truth. "Because he's my brother and I know him."

"We're fine, I swear." Nikole tried an unsuccessful 'convincing' laugh.

Kortney looked Nikole straight in the eyes. "The truth will set you free."

At that moment, Nikole wasn't easily convinced.

The girls brought the food and dishes to the table. As the night went on, everyone started bonding with Nikole. This made her feel a little better. She had stuff to get off her chest but just didn't know how at the time. She wasn't the only one who felt that way however. Tyrone had a huge announcement that would change their holiday family trip forever.

"I'm glad you all came," Tyrone said, talking to his adult children and their lovers. "I may have some terrible news depending on who you ask." Everyone was anxious. "Your Uncle Richard died." At that moment, a wave of silence came over the house. "There's more though . . ." He paused. "Your mother is on her way here."

"I hope you're talking about Deborah," Marquis said with hints of animosity. "That's the only mother I have!" he snapped like a little bitch.

"She hurt me too," Tyrone said, "she hurt all of us, but so did I. She should be here in the next ten minutes."

The three were shocked. The Smiths hadn't seen their mother in 19 years. Emotions ran through them like cocaine in the bloodstream. A silent rush shocked the room. Then someone opened the door.

Chapter Ten: Mother's Finally Home

As Cecily walked in, her children just stared. To them, it was like looking at a complete stranger. Cecily, once in her glory in beautiful sundresses, full of life and pizazz, was now in total discomposure. She wore an oversized sweater with grey jogging pants. Some of her teeth were missing and her hair was very thin with multiple bald spots. Cecily was nearly unrecognizable. When she walked toward her children, tears started to flow. Everyone in the room was trying to wrap their heads around the situation.

"Mama, is that you?" Kortney asked, tears silently streaming down her face. Kortney and Nick ran to hug her.

"Kids, your mother has been staying here for a while now." He put his arm around Marquis' shoulder. "Your uncle has actually been dead a couple of years."

Since Cecily and Richard lived so far away, the three had never bothered to visit or ask about them. But there was something about this reunion that didn't sit right with Marquis.

"Why do you look like a crackhead?" Marquis asked, looking down at his plate.

"Son," Tyrone slapped him upside the head, "that's still your mother!"

"I told you, my mother's name is Deborah . . ." Marquis paused and looked at her. "That woman there, is the one who abandoned me. That's Cecily."

Marquis stormed out the back door. As Cecily watched him leave, her heart sank. She knew she had not only cut a deep wound in his heart, but also in the hearts of the two who held her at that moment. Nothing she'd done had been worth losing them. She had never met any of her children's partners. All the money Cecily gained being with Richard had been depleted, and in its place, she'd gained scars of sexual, emotional, and physical abuse. 19 years of her life gone!

After 20 minutes the family knew Marquis had no plans on coming back. Mario thought for a second, and figured Marquis was at an old park where they used to spend time, so he set out to find his lover. Marquis sat under a tree with his phone to his face. As he spotted Mario approaching, he cleverly slipped the phone into his back pocket. Mario didn't even realize what had just happened.

"What's wrong?" He sat next to Marquis. "Why are you so mad?"

"You don't understand," Marquis responded evadingly, looking at cars as they passed by. "You chose not to be in your parents' lives. I was abandoned."

"It's different, I know, but the pain is still there." Mario took his hand. "I still love them though. And that's how Cecily feels."

"FUCK-HER-FEELINGS!" Marquis shouted. "SHE DIDN'T GIVE-A-DAMN ABOUT LOVE WHILE SHE WAS FUCKING MY UNCLE, DID SHE?"

"And Tyrone cheated also," he reminded Marquis. "They both have their pros and their cons. It's up to you to pick which traits you're going to focus on."

"At this point, I just want to be left alone." Marquis turned his back on Mario.

"This attitude you have is going to push people away from you, and more than likely Marqi, you'll need these people in the long run. So I'll leave you alone now, but I'll be here when you're ready to take a more positive approach to this situation."

A little hurt by Marquis's actions, Mario left and headed back to the house. Marquis waited until he was out of sight. Then he pulled his phone out and dialed a number.

"Hey, are you busy?' He asked the person on the phone.

"Nah bae, what's up?" Terrell replied.

Marquis told Terrell everything, all the things he should have been telling Mario. There was something about Terrell not being there that allowed Marquis to let his emotions out. It was an hour and a half conversation about Cecily and the affect the relationship, or lack thereof, had on him. Terrell didn't mind being a listening ear, especially since the sex over the past couple of months had been mind-blowing. They would meet at Marquis and Mario's apartment when Mario was in school. It wasn't just sex—it was love. It was like they had a connection that had been there forever. They weren't worried about the outside world. It was just the two of them. They ended the conversation with, "I love you."

❧ ◆ ☙

Back at the house, Kortney and Koko were in one of the four guest rooms. It had been Kortney's childhood bedroom. Posters of Kennan and Kel, All That, and That's So Raven still hung on her purple walls. A big Destiny's Child poster was still on the back of the door. They lay spooned on the bed.

"I don't know that woman." Kortney shook her head. "That can't be my mother. She would never leave the house looking like that."

"We shouldn't have come," Koko mentioned with hints of sarcasm.

"Why are you doing this? This isn't a time to be a smartass," Kortney said with a little force. "Sorry, but it's the truth. Those people have fucked you up enough."

"Well, those people are my family."

The tension in the couple's conversation escalated rather quickly. Koko made another point about how Kortney's parents had done nothing but mess her mind up. And, even though there was no harm behind her comments, Kortney took them to heart.

"Bitch, get the fuck out my face!"

Koko froze in disbelief. "Well then," Koko said gently. She left the room with Kortney lying on the bed crying.

"THIS IS WHY YOU DON'T DO DUMB SHIT LIKE THIS, NIKOLE!" Nick yelled at her in the dusty basement of his father's home that was filled with old items which had been accumulated over the years.

"Look, I'm sorry. It's just you never talk about your — "

"MAYBE THERE WAS A REASON FOR IT!", Nick spat, cutting her off.

"You know what's about to happen now, right?"

Nick motioned for her to get down on her knees. She began to crawl slowly towards him. Nick unzipped his pants with anticipation. When she finally got to him, he looked at her intensely. Then he slapped her. Trying to hold back tears, she did exactly what was expected. It was a routine. Whenever Nick felt disobeyed, he'd slap her face, then she'd begin to perform oral sex. If he still wasn't pleased, it would be cause for another 'punishment'. Even though Nikole hated him and could leave at any time, she'd convinced herself she needed Nick, no matter what.

Chapter Eleven: Mama Showed Me, Daddy Taught Me

On the last day at the house, the unhappy family mustered up enough tolerance to have one final meal together. Seafood gumbo with rice and corn muffins, and a sweet potato pie for dessert. Tyrone and Cecily had actually made the meal together. As the parents walked into the dining room, they could feel their children's confusion. Yet, they thought if they didn't say anything, neither would their children.

"Me and your father wanted to make sure you had a nice meal before you leave tomorrow," Cecily said, talking to the room.

It was hard to look at Cecily's fraily built body. She only weighed 90 pounds. Life with a multi- millionaire had been totally different from what she had expected.

"I guess we praying now, huh?" Marquis asked sarcastically.

"Just for that, you can pray, Marquis." Tyrone looked sternly at his son.

"Jesus wept. Amen." Marquis started to eat.

Mario stopped him.

"I'll pray."

Everyone was stunned to hear those words come out Cecily's mouth.

"God grant me the serenity to accept the things I cannot change, the courage to change the things I can, and the wisdom to know the difference. Help my children and my gracious husband see what you saw, and open up their hearts to give me a second chance . . ."

When everyone said, "Amen," Cecily dropped to the floor unconscious.

Pacing the county hospital ER waiting room, everyone was anxious to hear something. It had been two hours. Kortney, at that moment, wondered why things happened the way they did.

She knew someone had the answer to that. Her brothers enveloped her in a loving hug.

"Do you need anything, baby?" Koko asked Kortney.

"No; no, thank you." At that moment, it was hard for her to speak.

Marquis and Mario sat down across from each other. Marquis engaged himself with his phone, which annoyed the fuck out Mario.

"Are you really on the phone?" Mario whispered.

Marquis ignored him and kept his attention on his phone. It took all Mario's strength not to go off. Going off wasn't part of his personality and he sure didn't it want it to be in a moment like this.

Nikole sat down next to Nick, frightened. In her mind, she was the reason Cecily was in the hospital. If she had only left things alone, maybe the situation would have been resolved.

"Babe, are you okay?" Nikole asked as she held onto Nick's shoulder.

"Don't say another-fucking-word, all right?!" he hissed, shoving her away. His palms began to sweat.

A few moments later, a doctor came and took Tyrone to the side where no one could hear their conversation. Tyrone had always had a poker face that he used mostly to cover up his lies, but sometimes it covered up his emotions too. When the conversation was done, the doctor disappeared down the hospital hallway. The three gathered together to hear the words of their father.

"I have another confession." Tyrone swallowed his sadness. "Your mother had severe organ failure."

"Is she okay?" Kortney said, knowing the answer already.

"She's gone." Tyrone said as he hugged them.

In that moment, it seemed everything Cecily had done came back on her. All the money she'd gained had only brought temporary joy. The rest of her life had been hell— beat by her lover, separated from her husband, and unloved by her children. This was the example the Smith children had as a guide on how to be, and how to treat a lady. It was time they broke the unhealthy patterns passed from generation to generation.

Chapter Twelve: Never Can Say Goodbye

"I'm at my mother's funeral," Marquis said, talking to Terrell on the phone outside in front of the church.

He wore a blue suit with a pink tie like all the other men there. You could feel he was extremely uncomfortable. This was his first funeral and it was his mother's.

"Well, no, we weren't close, but I'd never hear the end of it if I didn't come." He paused to listen.

"I know, I wish you were here too."

The conversation went on a good ten minutes. All the while, everyone had been looking for Marquis.

"Why are you out here, honey?" Mario asked lovingly.

Marquis slid his phone into his suit pocket. "I'm fine."

Marquis took in a deep breath and sighed. "Just needed some fresh air, that's all." "Well, come in the family hour is almost over."

The two entered the sanctuary as people stared at them. Some gazed, feeling their pain, and the others peered in disapproval.

"Hell fire and brimstone for those two," they heard a mother of the church say.

"A walking abomination," one elder said.

When they made it to their seats, the service began. It had been hard to find a willing minister to give the eulogy given the family's 'unusual' life. However, Deborah was able to convince the Pastor at her church. When the minister spoke, it felt like satan himself had taken the mic. Every single word was a lie. He made Cecily seem so innocent.

"Cecily Lailah Smith was an endearing wife and mother."

There was no truth behind his words. She was now just a memory of a sad life lived. Yes, she had suffered, but had she suffered in vain or had she gotten what she deserved? Whatever the case, ashes to ashes, dust to dust was Cecily's final outcome on this earth.

The repast was mostly made up of Tyrone's friends and some of the church congregation. Cecily's family had abandoned her long ago. Deborah, godmother to all three Smith children, and childhood friend of Cecily, had made most of the food. She even fixed their plates.

Deborah was small, round, and fluffy. She wore glasses and had three distinctive moles on her face. She had a tendency to wobble when she walked. When she finally got to the family table, she took a couple of heavy breaths.

"How you holdin' up, babes?" She leaned in toward them. "I'm glad you all got to see her one last time. I know it's hard to digest, but truth is, all she knew how to do was run away. That's all anyone taught her."

This was the first truthful thing anyone had said to them all week. The Smiths weren't a religious family, yet they still wondered if there was a heaven or hell, and if so, which place was their mother in?

PART THREE

PART THREE

Chapter Thirteen: Back to Life, Back to Reality

When Kortney and Koko got back to New York, things were crazy. Seeing her mom after 19 years of abandonment, then her dying right next to her, was a lot for Kortney to process. Neither of them knew how to go about life any more. These ladies weren't the grieving type. They weren't taught to grieve, they were taught to push, and Kortney pushed the best way she could. She went back to pursuing her dream of performing on Broadway while Koko dealt with everything else—which meant sex was very rare. That wasn't something Koko enjoyed. Koko's 'friend' Tangya was all too willing to help her out with anything she needed when Kortney wasn't around. Tangya was her secret acquaintance. Koko booked her gigs, introduce her to business friends, and from time to time, got paid for it. Not with money, but with the great luxury she wasn't getting from Kortney—sex.

It wasn't love, passion, or romance—it was just sex. As long as it was just sex, everything was cool. At least for Koko. But Tangya saw it as more than sex. It was everything to her that it wasn't for Koko. The only problem was Kortney. If only Tangya could get rid of her, she and Koko could be together. Even if she was the only one who actually saw it happening.

The hundredth audition of the year. With every callback, Kortney became more of herself. However, the "no's" and 'not this time's "bothered her to a point of sadness, a sadness that slowly morphed into rage. Her rage pushed Koko closer and closer to Tangya's vagina.

Kortney would leave the house, cursing and yelling at her wife. Koko never argued back, but her revenge and forgiveness came from fucking Tangya. Tangya was the person keeping Koko and Kortney together—and, at the same time, pulling them apart. The reality of it all was a disconnected love triangle. Tangya now had the upper hand and she planned to use Koko like a pawn.

Chapter Fourteen: I Want Someone I Don't Need

Hip to hip, chest to chest, mouth to mouth. Everything he wanted was provided for him by a man he shouldn't have been with. Marquis and Mario were back to their routine. Mario went to school while Marquis went to model and act, but not without having deep personal, sexual, and intense conversations with Terrell, the man Marquis really connected with.

"Why am I so in love with you?" Marquis asked on a phone call with Terrell. "I've never felt this way before."

"You need a listening ear," Terrell said, "and I'm here for you."

"I know, but I shouldn't be talking to you," Marquis said, feeling guilty. "I tell you things I don't tell Mario."

"And I say the things Mario doesn't say to you," Terrell said, trying to make Marquis not feel guilty.

The truth was, that even though they were having a physical relationship, it was primarily the mental and emotional relationship that had a hold on Marquis, a relationship that made them cum off of each other's words. Terrell was there for Marquis when Mario couldn't be. The thing was hiding his attraction for another person. When Mario made love to him, all he could think about was Terrell, to the point he would stay silent during sex in fear he would call out Terrell's name.

The phone alarm went off. In a hurry to wake Mario up, Marquis shook him, but Mario pushed him away.

"Baby, it's 7:30," Marquis said.

"Marqi, class is canceled today," Mario said, half sleep. "Our instructor had a conference."

"Okay," Marquis said hesitantly.

"You want to go out, Marqi?"

"I would but I have auditions."

Marquis didn't have an audition, rather, a date with Terrell later. With Mario having the day off, it messed up Marquis' routine. How would he see Terrell without Mario knowing?

"No study groups?" Marquis asked with a touch of hope.

"No, Marqi, I know I've been gone a lot," Mario responded, feeling guilty, "but I have to take care of my man, right?"

"Right."

Marquis received a text on his phone.

"Hey baby"

Marquis instantly put the phone down so he wouldn't have to explain everything. It was Terrell. He knew his schedule, but with Mario around for the day, it complicated things.

"Who was that, Marqi?"

"That was the agency." Marquis could always come up with a quick cover up. "They want me there in an hour."

"Really? I was hoping I could make breakfast in bed." Mario started to pull on Marqi's underwear. "Don't you wanna feed me?"

Mario started to touch, kiss, lick, and more. Marquis couldn't handle it; his sexual desire took over. Mario covered and kissed everything. He gave the best head Marquis would ever have. Marquis lay in the bed naked, moaning, crying, and enjoying. But, at the same time, he felt guilty because all he could think about was Terrell.

When Mario finished, Marquis headed to the bathroom. This gave him a chance to text Terrell. Marquis felt guilty for thinking about another man during sex. He couldn't get to the shower fast enough. He washed his wants, needs, and desires away.

Later that morning, when Mario left to run a few errands, it was the perfect time to call Terrell. Marquis was contemplating ending their romance. He thought about Mario and all the years they had been together. Still, Marquis was afraid of how Terrell would feel. He knew Terrell loved him, but didn't want to end up like his parents—loveless. He took his phone and dialed Terrell's number.

"We have to talk . . ."

Things in L.A. weren't all glitz and glamour. In reality, they had just gotten worse. As Mario pulled up to his school, he recognized a man. His ex-boyfriend was standing by the entrance to the building. Mario slowly approached him.

"Terrell," Mario said, "what are you doing here?"

"I'm enrolling, thought it was time to go back." Terrell lied.

Mario couldn't help the shocked look on his face. They had been broken up almost eight years now.

"What made you come to Cali?" Mario asked.

"Cincinnati just wasn't cutting it." Terrell sighed. "Needed new scenery. How've you been?"

"Busy. This place might as well be my home," Mario joked. "You single?"

"Yeah, ever since you dumped me!"

"I didn't dump you." Mario chuckled. "We just went in separate directions."

"Yeah, how about you? Single?"

"No. Remember Marquis?"

"From drama club?"

"Yep, I'm with him."

Mario and Terrell's conversation lasted a good six minutes. Terrell secretly enjoyed fucking with people's minds. He had Marquis...now to get Mario back. Terrell hadn't gotten over the fact that Mario had fallen out of love with him. He didn't love or want Marquis. He just wanted Mario back and all to himself. Marquis was a pawn in a fucked-up Chess game to reconquer the love of his life... Mario!

"Why don't you come over?" Mario asked. "Marquis loves having people over."

"Sounds great."

They exchanged numbers. Mario ran to class, while Terrell called and checked on Marquis. All hell was about to break loose. Terrell knew exactly what he was doing. It was, 'If I can't have you, I'll take the one who does.'

ဗာ◆ၜာ

Later that night, Marquis, feeling guilty about his secret affair, decided to make a nice dinner for him and Mario, not knowing a guest was coming to dinner. When Mario walked in, he could smell the food cooking—chicken, with baked sweet potatoes, steamed cheese broccoli, and a red velvet cake.

"Hey, bae." Mario greeted Marquis with a kiss. "You've got it smelling good in here."

"I try." Marquis blushed a bit.

"I hope you don't mind. I ran into an old friend from high school and invited him to dinner." "Of course not. Who is it?"

"Remember Terrell?"

Marquis froze in fear. When he heard the name Terrell, it was like time stopped. Marquis took a deep breath.

"Terrell?"

"Yeah, you probably don't remember him." Marquis wished in that moment he didn't. "He actually doesn't live that far away," Mario said. "I'm going to change. Listen out for the door."

Mario vanished in the room, leaving Marquis in shock. Marquis' mind and heart were going hundreds of miles per minute. He realized all Terrell was there for was to 'get in the way'. Moments later, there was a knock on the door. Marquis hesitantly opened the door to see a big grin on Terrell's face.

"Hey, I'm Terrell." He slapped Marquis on the ass.

"What-the-fuck are you doing?"

"What a way to treat company."

Before Marquis could voice another thought, Mario re-entered the room. "Hey, Terrell." Mario hugged him. "You remember Marquis, don't you?"

"I sure do," he replied.

"Everyone hungry?" Marquis asked, trying to speed the evening up.

Terrell sat in the middle of the two. Most of the dinner consisted of an A-and-B conversation between Terrell and Mario, while Terrell secretly touched Marquis in sensitive areas underneath the table. Marquis did his best to ignore the sexual acts and keep a poker face.

Finally, dinner was over, but Marquis knew something else was coming.

"We should all hang out sometime!" Mario suggested.

"Sounds great!" Terrell winked at Marquis.

"I'll have to check my schedule . . ." Marquis added.

"We can hang at night, Marqi," Mario said.

"Great! You have my number, just call me," Terrell said as he walked out the door.

As soon as the door shut, Marquis let out a sigh of relief. All he wanted to do now was sleep, but Mario had different plans. Marquis was in no way in a sexual state of mind, but that didn't stop Mario. It was dessert time.

Chapter Fifteen: Is This Really Love

Things in Atlanta had gotten fiery! The death of Nick's mother weighed heavily on him. Nikole thought she was the one bringing all the unwanted emotions and memories to Nick. Nick had become more violent and cold. He had gotten fired from the modeling agency he and Nikole were signed to, and now it was up to her to take care of him. She bought groceries, cooked, cleaned, and fucked him, while he talked down to and abused her.

"WHAT'S TAKING YOUR ASS SO LONG?" Nick yelled to Nikole. "I'M HUNGRY!"

Nikole stood in the kitchen crying while he yelled. She thought about leaving from time to time, but she was in love. It was hard for her to ask herself, "Is this really love?" Nick was all she had. Everyone else was gone.

Santa Barbara, California May 2, 2000 ~

Nikole's mother Janet was applying makeup to her young face. They were in a bathroom the size of a house. Janet was an aspiring model who'd never made it, but she was determined to make Nikole a star— even if she didn't want to be one.

"Mommy, I don't want makeup," a young Nikole whined. "Why do I need it?"

"Because you're ugly without it." Janet hugged her. "You want to be pretty, right?"

"Yes," Nikole said, tears flowing down her face.

"Then you'd better not fuck-up your makeup!" Janet said, walking away.

That was the example Nikole had growing up. It made Nikole always put beauty before everything. It was the most important thing to her. Before faith, money, or love, it was beauty. She had never been presented with the tools a woman needed to live in the craziness of life. Nikole was a woman who'd never been taught what it truly meant to love—or be loved.

Nick was sitting on the couch in the dark where he scrolled mindlessly through his phone wearing nothing but a white T-shirt and boxers.

"BAE!" Nick yelled to Nikole as she walked through the small studio door carrying bags of groceries. "WHERE YOU BEEN, GIRL?"

"There was a long line." Nikole sighed. "Why is it so dark? Why are the candles all lit?"

She thought maybe Nick was doing something special for a change. Then, Nikole flipped the switch, and nothing happened. She looked over at the pile of mail next to Nick. He hadn't paid any of the bills. With her being the only one working, she depended on Nick to at least make sure the bills were paid. He had access to her account, but he was spending money on non-essential items.

Nick ignored her questions. In six months, Nikole's love for Nick had literally shut her life down. She feared if she questioned him any further, he might possibly kill her. She feared him just as she'd feared her mother, reprimanded for all the things she did wrong. Nikole lived a fearful, painful, and loveless life.

"You didn't pay the bills?" Nikole asked Nick calmly. "Babe?"

'I forgot, damn!" he replied, not looking up from his phone.

"I can't do this, Nick." Nikole dropped her bags. "What happened? Six months ago, we were happy. Nick, you and I were happy! What happened?"

Nikole felt tears rain down her face. She could feel her body boiling with anger. Deep slow breaths was what she thought about as she slowly approached Nick.

"Babe, I'm sorry," Nick stood up and embraced her. "I just haven't been okay since I've come back." Nick started to get extremely emotional.

Nikole was shocked, He had never cried or showed any deep emotions. Nikole now saw Nick needed her; just as much as she needed him. She just couldn't leave.

Chapter Sixteen: Thought You Should Know

Koko was back in the studio with her prodigy Tangya. The studio was small, in an old building, and only fifty dollars an hour. It was Koko's escape from the home drama, and Tangya was Koko's physical escape. They were in the studio almost every day—sometimes recording and smoking, and other times . . . fucking. Koko didn't think about Kortney, but Tangya did. "She's going to find out," she said as Koko kissed her neck while they sat on the couch. "Don't you feel guilty?"

"T, calm down," Koko said, frustrated. "She knows I'm in the booth. Chill!" Koko tried to keep pleasuring her, but Tangya slowly pushed her away. "I can't do this."

"What do you mean, you can't?" Koko took a breath. "We do this all the time."

The next day Tangya sat in the recording studio, she had gotten deeper in her feelings. Tangya's conscience was filled to capacity with guilt, or at least, that is what she wanted Koko to think. She decided to call Kortney. It was the only way to make her move. But, before she could call, her phone rang.

"Hello?" Tangya answered her phone.

"Hey. Is this Tangya?"

"Who's this?"

"Don't worry about who I am. I asked if this is Tangya," the caller snapped back. "Yes, and who are you?"

"Kaira's wife," Kortney said.

Now that Tangya had her chance to come clean, she questioned her desire. There was no going back now.

"Listen," Tangya said, trying to explain her situation. "I feel bad—"

"Bitch, I don't give a fuck about yo' feelings!" Kortney was heated. "I don't blame you though. Kaira ain't shit!"

Tangya was so confused. 'Is this really happening?' Then something unexpected happened. Suddenly Tangya heard yelling on the line.

"What-the-fuck are you doin'?" It was Koko yelling at Kortney.

"I'm talking to your little fuck-buddy you're trying to hide!" Kortney looked at her. "You be 'recording', huh?"

"Why you trippin'?" Koko asked. "We're friends."

"Let me ask the bitch." Kortney put the phone on speaker. "You just friends?" Kortney asked Tangya.

SILENCE.

"You gonna answer?!"

Tangya froze.

"Baby, calm down." Koko made her way over to Kortney. "Chill."

"GET OUT!"

As Koko tried to touch her, Kortney shoved her.

"I SAID LEAVE, WITH YOUR LYING-ASS!" Kortney turned red. "BYE TO YOU AND YOUR BITCH!"

Koko quickly went to the bathroom, packed clothes in an overnight bag and left, leaving Kortney heated. Kortney's rage made her grab a hammer out the closet and demolish all of Koko's recording equipment, then she cried. Her tears turned to fire and fury. She'd had enough of Koko!

PART FOUR:
THE UNEXPECTED
CONCLUSION

Chapter Seventeen: Break Ups Are Forever

When Nick fell asleep after a night of mind-blowing sex— for him at least—Nikole lay in the bed and started to become angry. Anger consumed her mind, body, and spirit. At that moment, she knew her purpose in his life and didn't like it. Nikole was about to do something very unexpected . . . She left.

12:47 AM. Nick woke up with a big yawn and stretched.

"Yo, bae." He looked over and noticed Nikole wasn't in bed. "Bae . . . BAE?!"

Nick became furious. His whole body was covered in sweat. He searched the small studio, still no Nikole. Nick picked up his phone and called her. It went straight to voicemail. "Bitch, where-the-fuck are you? You know yo'-ass can't leave without permission. I got somethin' for that-ass when you get back!"

He sat bewildered that another woman had left him. Nick thought over the last year. Regrets suddenly filled his brain like poisonous fluid— as well as every bad trait that had been passed on to him. He thought about Nikole and all the hurt he'd put on her in a year. Once a young, fabulous, happy girl with her whole career ahead of her, Nikole had now been stopped by a man incapable of loving. He had to make amends.

❧◆❧

Five hours later, Nikole walked back in the door and was shocked. Nick had done something, something sweet.

"What's this?" she asked.

"An 'I'm sorry' dinner." He motioned for her to take her seat. "I'm not perfect."

Nikole sat at the table with a blank expression. It was unexpected he would try to fix anything. She had mixed emotions the whole dinner. Finally, the next move. After dinner, Nick wanted to show his gratitude in a way that would thrill Nikole to the point of no return. It was three easy steps. Nick convinced Nikole he was truly sorry. Nikole did what she always did. Forgive him. Nick wanted to show his gratitude in a way she'd never forget. He laid her body down in the bed and started to fuck her like never before.

They lay together in the heat of the moment, tensions high, bodies sweating, hearts pounding. It was the beginning of a mystifying night. Scared yet excited, passionate yet strong, love in the beginning can never be wrong. In a room just big enough for two, they started to connect in a way that felt inhuman. As they began on an unknown path they'd never before seen, it became clear they were no longer in control. The fight to gain back that control slowly died and the tears in their eyes became proof of inseparable love. Suddenly, His hands began to slide around her neck. While still making love, Nick beat her head in, again, and again, and again... until blood crawled like snakes slithering down the wall and onto the bed.

Nick hurried to clean himself up. He knew he couldn't handle being left by her again. In a span of five hours Nick had a plane ticket to a destination where no one would think to find him. He knew Nikole had money hidden in an audition packet. All the bills were in her name, and the only ones who knew about their relationship were his dysfunctional family. He wasn't worried, and actually became a ghost by starting a life on Isla Mujeres off the coast of Mexico. But first, Nick needed to snap one more picture of Nikole. He took it, of course, with his camera.

Chapter Eighteen: You Thought You Knew Me

Kortney now gave zero fucks. After ruining all the studio equipment, she then went after Koko's Clothing.

"I threw all your shit out!" Kortney said in a text.

Koko was now living with Tangya and everything was going great—until Tangya started to become needy. Suddenly, it was like she couldn't do anything for herself. Koko wasn't use to having to baby someone. Whining and begging was all Koko heard now. When things didn't go her way, Tangya would have fits worse than a toddler. Koko was ready to bounce, but the sad truth was, she had nowhere to go. As time moved on, Koko started to realize how stupid she was acting. She couldn't justify any of her actions and that made her bitter. She was now in this fantastic sexual relationship with a person she hated. What should she do? Koko would do the thing she'd known so well—leave!

Tangya started noticing Kortney's things being packed up bit-by-bit. "Where you going?" Tangya asked.

"I'm leaving," Koko said, with no emotion. "Thanks, but this isn't working out."

"No . . ." she started to whine.

"See, That's the shit I'm talking about." Tangya ran to Koko on her knees.

"Are you a dog or something?" Koko asked, kicking her out the way as she headed to the door.

All Tangya could do was cry as Koko left. But, if Koko thought leaving her would be that easy, she had another think coming.

After Koko begged Kortney for mercy and Kortney cursed her out a few times, the two were back together. They decided to do whatever it would take to mend their marriage. Koko finally got a paid gig as a studio engineer. Everything was fine . . . Until one day, Kortney was at home and got a bad feeling. Then her phone rang.

"Hello?" Kortney answered.

"Your bitch is mine!" the caller said.

"Who-the-fuck is this?"

"The bitch that keeps your wife moaning and groaning!"

"I'm about to ask you one more time . . . This bet' not be Tangya."

"I will kill you and Koko!" Tangya hung up the phone.

Kortney was furious. She wanted Koko to fix it and fix it now!

Since Koko and Tangya had a binding musical agreement together they were stuck, and being stuck was a problem, and even more so of a problem was Tangya. . She knew how to trap Koko. They would record for a while until she got 'tired' and needed to take a 'break'. Then she would try to seduce Koko. But nothing worked . . . except head. It got her every time.

Koko was quick to get undressed. Her stress lessened when Tangya's tongue entered her. Screams of love were released. Tangya was prepared as she gave Koko a strap-on to fuck her with. As wrong as it was, Koko couldn't resist. Just when Tangya thought it was through, another thrust was given. As her brain entered a tizzy, she couldn't help but think, 'Damn, she's good!' She surrendered to the love of her passionate partner.

Then Kortney entered.

Not only did she enter the room with anger, but with a metal bat. She commenced to breaking everything in the studio—including Koko. Tangya ran out like a little-bitch before Kortney could get to her. It was Koko vs. Kortney. Every time Koko screamed, she beat her harder. Kortney wasn't beating her just for cheating, Kortney beat Koko for everything bad that had happened to her: her mother not being there the majority of her life, and all the no's she'd received on auditions that held her back from her dreams of making it as a Broadway actress. Abruptly, Kortney stopped beating Koko, as killing her wasn't the goal. Kortney just wanted Koko to hurt physically as bad as she did emotionally.

"I forgive you," Kortney said, helping Koko to the car to go to the hospital.

"Thank you," was all Koko could say as her eyes closed and her head banged against the dashboard.

Fear, panic, and sadness took over Kortney, her wife's breath was very faint.

"You won't go alone . . ."

Kortney spun out and their car dived into the cold Hudson River . . .

Chapter Nineteen: The Drive-In

Mario and Terrell had been spending a lot of time together without Marquis— it wasn't that Mario wanted to be alone with Terrell, but Marquis always refused to hang out because he was now uncomfortable around his secret lover. Marquis knew that if he didn't break up this rekindled friendship between Terrell and Mario, secrets were bound to come out. Marquis thought it was time to talk to Mario.

"Babe, why do you spend so much time alone with Terrell?" Marquis asked boldly.

"What do you mean? You're the one who always declines to go with us," Mario said as he packed-up for school. "And, he's an ex for a reason."

"I DON'T LIKE IT!" he yelled, reflecting all his guilt onto Mario.

"What the hell is wrong with you?" Mario asked. "Look, I'm late for school. I'll call you between classes.

As Mario left out the door, Marquis started to cry. He realized he was in love with a man who wasn't his.

One day, Terrell asked the guys to go to a drive-in. Of course, Marquis said no. Not because he didn't want to go, he just didn't want to go with them.

When the guys left, Marquis waited a moment then followed them. On his secret mission, he saw they had parked in the middle of the lot, so Marquis spied from the back. The movie went on and nothing out of the ordinary happened—until Terrell disappeared out of his sightline. So much ran through Marquis's mind, like water falling off a cliff.

He imagined Terrell starting slowly, his purpose to please Mario. Mario was moaning as he pleasured him in a way no one else could. The repeated motion made them both hot. Wanting the same outcome, they worked together to feel, build a climax, simply make love.

But, a problem occurred, a problem they'd neither seen nor felt. Pleasure slowly turned to pain.

The two stopped when they felt the presence of someone else. Someone was pulled out the car. They both screamed in panic. Suddenly, one started gasping for air. It was over . . . he was dead.

"WHAT DID YOU DO?!" Mario screamed.

Without realizing what he was doing, Marquis had choked Terrell to death.

"WHAT'S WRONG WITH YOU?!"

Marquis stood there, realizing nothing sexual had happened. It had all been in his mind.

Conclusion: What Not To Do

Each person in this story had their own demons to tame. The lesson I wanted to convey is simple: "You can't be fully committed or happy in a relationship until you understand who you are first." Life doesn't always need to be immediate. Life is a process, and that process is what makes you. If you rush the process you won't learn. If you don't learn. you'll eventually become insane. The definition of insanity is doing the same thing and expecting a new result.

You might not be as crazy as the couples in the story, but we all have our quirks. So don't be scared to relate to these people; then learn from them.

CPSIA information can be obtained
at www.ICGtesting.com
Printed in the USA
JSHW030454130421
13517JS00008B/55